THE BOAT OF MANY ROOMS

THE BOAT OF MANY ROOMS

THE STORY OF NOAH IN VERSE

BY J. PATRICK LEWIS

ILLUSTRATED BY REG CARTWRIGHT

ATHENEUM BOOKS FOR YOUNG READERS

Once long ago the world turned wicked.
People everywhere had become so cruel
that God decided to put an end
to the human race
and begin again.

This is the story of Noah,
the last good man on earth—
the story of the great flood
and how Noah, his family, and the animals
survived on the boat of many rooms.

God, raging in His heaven,
    Surveyed the wretched earth
And wept to see humanity
    To which He'd given birth.

Though Noah's heart was humble,
    He who was without blame
Knew all along to right the wrong
    That God might call his name.

"Bring Shem and Ham and Japheth,
    Your sons," God bid him well.
"And build an ark to weather
    Fierce winds and the long sea swell.
Bring fortitude and patience,
    Leave your wealth behind,
And make room for the animals—
    A pair of every kind.

"For I shall raise the oceans
    To heights that reach the sky.
Neither thief nor sinner
    Shall live to wonder why
Black waters rage and swallow
    Every last hill and vale!
Only your people, Noah,
    Shall live to tell this tale."

From dawn to dark
they built an ark
of gopher wood and tar
and many a night
Noah worked by the light
of the last great evening star.

Three decks and the roof
were waterproof,
likewise the deep-bellied hold,
to protect the crew
and the cruising zoo
from the wind-whipped sea and the cold.

Noah's wife and sons
unloaded tons
of vegetables, nuts and fruits,
like figs and pears
for pigs and bears,
giraffes and bandicoots.

When the shipboard store
would hold no more
cucumbers, lentils, grain,
the crew was through—
and a good thing too—
for the clouds grew fat with rain.

"All animals aboard!" cried Noah.
"From pachyderms to protozoa!

Welcome frog, and welcome toad,
to lily pads in my abode!

Birds of paradise, see if you can
Fit between the coot and toucan.

Mr. and Mrs. Mole, would you
Share a room with the kinkajou?

After the pussycat couple arrives,
Birds to the rafters, bees to the hives.

Hurry up the gangplank, mice,
Hippos, armadillos! Twice

A day we'll serve you oats and peas.
Crocodiles, would you *please*

Settle down as we prepare
To put to sea? Now don't despair,
But kindly say a little prayer. . . ."

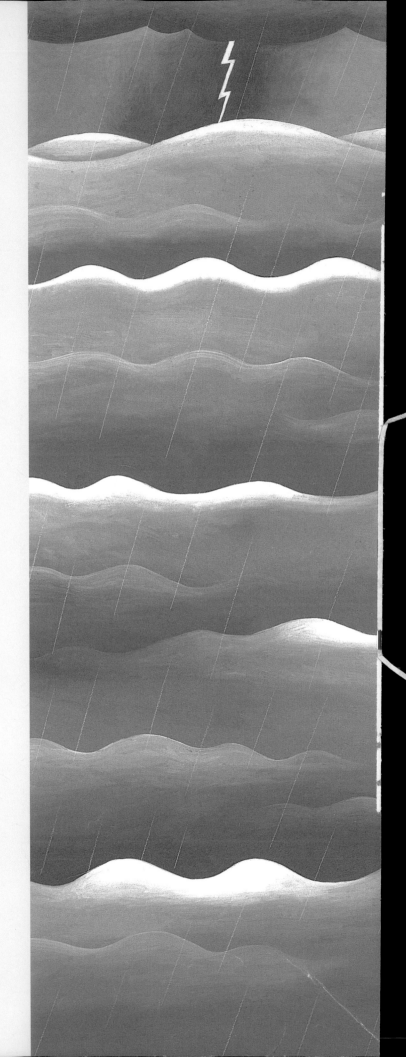

For days it rained
        As Heaven wept
Torrential tears,
        And no one slept.
When flood tides rose,
        Blue mountains lost
Their silvered peaks.
        The ark was tossed
So violently
        Birds beat their wings.
Fear cornered all
        Four-footed things.
The wives of Japheth,
        Ham and Shem
Sang lullabies
        To comfort them
From the monotonous
        Symphony
Of pounding rain
        And sounding sea.

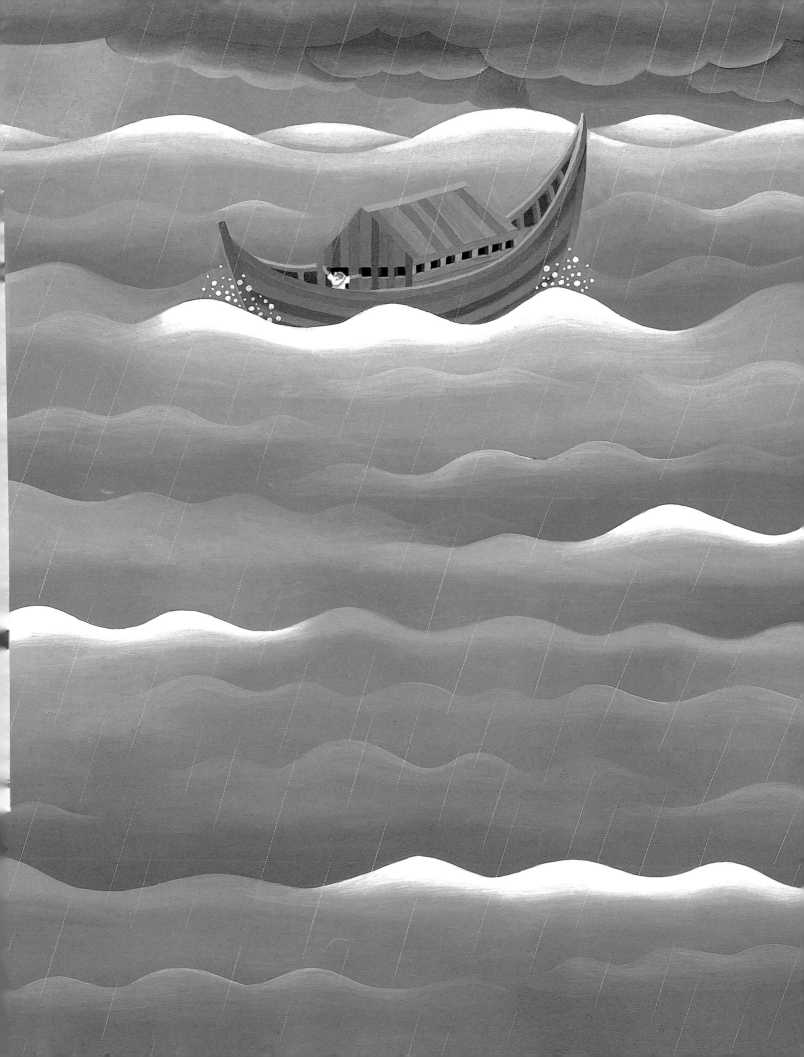

Flamingoes on the afterdeck,
　　Parrots along the rail
Whistled at the water dancing
　　Out of the booming gale.

The weasel's wife, to pass the time,
　　Pretended to make hay,
But listened carefully to what
　　The magpies had to say,

Which was to tell the ostriches,
　　"You shouldn't think it odd,
But Captain Noah means to do
　　The handiwork of God."

With that the peeps and plovers piped
　　A melody so sweet,
A rhino nudged a rabbit who
　　Began to tap her feet.

Gorillas beat the barrel drums
　　Softly. And beautiful plumes
Of peacock came parading through
　　The boat of many rooms!

One sea-gray day,
A hummingbird lay
In the palm of Noah's hand.
She seemed a bit
Disconsolate—
There were no trees, no land.

"Remember, bird,
God gave His word,"
Said Noah. "Though rains have poured,
My little friend,
All this will end.
So let us praise the Lord."

Five oceans took dominion
    Of earth for half a year
And made of waves a wilderness
    That would not disappear.

Then God took thought for Noah,
    And stilled His heavenly cup,
Commanding Wind to blow and Sun
    To drink the waters up.

The Sun, who was out of practice,
    Did the best it could,
Beaming on a watery world
    And a boat of gopher wood.

The Wind swept up the waters
    And laid the ark to rest
Upon a peak called Ararat,
    The mountain God had blessed.

Gracenotes fell from the cypress beams.
The women called back to birds above,
"Follow the raven, turtle dove!
Find the long lost land of our dreams."

The dove that flew from Noah's hand,
Sailing swiftly out of sight,
Came back weary late one night
Without so much as a grain of sand.

Seven days passed. Over the reef,
The white dove flew away once more. . . .
Returning from some distant shore,
She held in her mouth an olive leaf!

These things the Good Lord said to Noah:
The waters have subsided. Call all the animals
To the New World made.
Let the red fox quicken the seasons.
Let the zebra buck and clatter in the cage of his skin.
Let butterflies announce their colors to applause.
Leave the glass lagoons to the blue heron, whose eye is steady.
Let jungles whisper jaguar, whose paw is velvet.
Let the worm explore the globe, his apple.
Let the spider embroider the air.
Let the bat acrobats tumble till dawn.
Let the lowly slug pearl the footpaths of Asia Minor.
Let seagulls snow down the harbors of the East.
Let the panther surround the quiet panic she has made.
Let the hippos squat and the antelope lope.
Let the rhino bully the bush.
Let the turtle be.
Let the snail nod in the hush of her mushroom room.
Leave the deserts to the one- and the two-humped emperors.
Let the black kite brown the morning mustard fields.
Leave afternoons for music, the bees drilling in the lindens.
Let owls be your night lanterns, geese your compass, skunks your caution.

Up from the damp, deep-bellied dark,
The passengers filed to disembark
Out of the hatch on Noah's ark—
        Oh, was the green grass blowing!

Some sniffed the air and wiggled their toes,
Or shook the wrinkles out of their clothes.
And some ran wild, like the buffaloes,
        There on the green grass blowing.

Iguana, mongoose, mink and fox
Ran crazily across dry docks
Of fields and flowers, trees and rocks!
        Look at the green grass blowing.

Porcupine, milk cow, tiger, boa
Constrictor, two-toed sloth, and oh! a
Parade of animals followed Noah—
        Where? To the green grass blowing.

"Hark!" the Breath of Heaven thundered,
        "This is my covenant with you,
With all the children of your children,
        And with the universal zoo:

"Mark my word, Noah, that I shall never
        Destroy the earth by flood and rain.
This world I washed away in anger
        I now give back to you again.

"There's the reminder of my promise—
        A rainbow decorates the sky!
Bountiful earth is yours. Be fruitful,
        Increase your numbers! Multiply. . . ."

. . .and so they did
as God had bid.

For my Aunt Marion and Uncle Guido
—J. P. L.

For my brother Geoff, 1942–1995
—R. C.

Atheneum Books for Young Readers
An imprint of Simon & Schuster Children's Publishing Division
1230 Avenue of the Americas
New York, New York 10020

Book design by Michael Nelson

The text of this book is set in Adobe Usherwood.
The illustrations are rendered in oil paint.

First Edition
Printed in the United States of America
10   9   8   7   6   5   4   3   2   1

Library of Congress Cataloging-in-Publication Data
Lewis, J. Patrick.
The boat of many rooms / by J. Patrick Lewis ; illustrated by Reg Cartwright.—1st ed.
p.   cm.
Summary: Retells in verse the story of Noah's ark which saves two of every
kind of animal while a flood purges the earth.
ISBN: 0-689-80118-1
1. Noah (Biblical figure)—Juvenile fiction. [1. Noah (Biblical figure)—Fiction.
2. Noah's ark—Fiction. 3. Animals—Fiction. 4. Stories in rhyme.]
I. Cartwright, Reg, ill.   II. Title.
Pz8.3.L5855Bo 1997
[E]—dc20
95-581